GOD IN A CAN

ROBERT SCOTELLARO

BAMBOO
DART
PRESS

LOS ANGELES † NEW YORK † LONDON † MELBOURNE

God in a Can by Robert Scotellaro

ISBN: 978-1-947240-43-8

eISBN: 978-1-947240-44-5

First Printing 2022

Cover art by Dennis Callaci

Layout and design by Mark Givens

For information:

Bamboo Dart Press

chapbooks@bamboodartpress.com

Bamboo Dart Press 019

www.pelekinesis.com

www.bamboodartpress.com

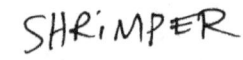
www.shrimperrecords.com

for Diana

ACKNOWLEDGMENTS

Grateful acknowledgment is made to the following publications in which these stories or earlier versions previously appeared:

"Sumo Wrestler's Heating Service" *Meniscus; Best Microfiction 2020*

"The Metamorphosis (Revisited)" *Flash Frontier; Nothing Is Ever One Thing*

"Kidnapped By Extravagant Poets" *Mad Swirl*

"Cloud Walkers" *Willows Wept Review*

"The Limits of Art" *Eclectic Flash Literary Journal; The Best of Eclectic Flash Anthology; Measuring the Distance*

"Simple Directions for Assembling an Existential Angst" *The Prose-Poem Project*

"Mime with a Gun" *Measuring the Distance*

"I See You" *Six Sentences*

"Crooners in the Web" *The Linnet's Wings; Measuring the Distance*

"Smooth Ride" *Mud Luscious*

"Safety Paper" *Clockwise Cat*

"Tuxedo Epiphany" *Measuring the Distance*

"The Sad Mirage of Metaphor and Mirage" *Clockwise Cat*

CONTENTS

"Only by living absurdly is it possible to break out of this infinite absurdity."
—Julio Cortázar

THAT'S WHEN WE'LL HEAR THE BIRDS SING

The giant "nagging clocks," as they've come to be known, are screaming out from every room at me. I will only be a bit late. But that is still enough to excite them. *My god, the epithets.* This is technological abuse. I hurry out, leave them belligerently hounding in my wake.

* * *

At the fortune cookie company where I work there are hundreds of cubicles like a sliced open hive, and we are hitting our keyboards furiously. Are rotated daily, so I don't know where Cassandra is. We are all "composers." Make up the esoteric tidbits that will be at the heart of those sugary shells to crack open. They are no longer the pat maxims we had before *The Great Ennui.* Now the "Others" want something *brain-challenging, abstruse.* Every household will have a copious supply of fortune cookies delivered as regularly as heartbeats. I've written two so far: *It is wise to note there are only exclamation points in a wrecking ball's grammar.* And: *Life is a beverage best sucked through a paper straw that keeps collapsing.* I'm hoping they'll be keepers. I get up and peek over the flimsy cubicle like so many others, hoping to glimpse a loved one. We stand there with the jittery vigilance of meerkats. I spot Cassandra for an instant, nearly in a blur, as she waves then shoots back down.

* * *

I head over to Cassandra's place after work. We go out back with a bowl of popcorn to watch the lemons yellow. We are giddy with adventure. I once cracked a tooth on an unpopped kernel. We decide to live dangerously. "If we are patient and don't fret, that's when we'll hear the birds sing," Cassandra tells me. It's become increasingly difficult to determine the difference between what we write for the "Others" and what we say to each other. Above us the sky is a wide-open purse and soon enough that one bright coin will drop out into the sea, and the crickets will be warming up their lovely instruments. We can hardly wait. A bit unruly, we've turned all the giant clocks around to face the wall, and have concluded because of it, in this moment, we just might live forever.

THE METAMORPHOSIS
(REVISITED)

He awakes to find he is a *thingamajig*. Some indeterminable gizmo. There is a cog (of sorts) where his stomach should be. Oddly enough it growls.

"Holy crap!" he says, looking into the dresser mirror. He clinks out to the kitchen where his wife is sipping her coffee and reading the paper. He has a crank and a nondescript lever, a doohickey of some kind with a flexible joint. He points at himself. "Madge," he says, "What the hell?"

His wife looks up and appraises him. "Hmm," she says. "I wonder what that Finnegan pin does. This might not be so bad, Fred–depending."

"Depending?" he screeches. "Depending on what?"

"Well, you never know what might come in handy. It might take some time to figure it all out. But, I think you've got a lot of potential here."

"But I'm a...*whatchamacallit.*"

She reaches over and presses a button. Something begins turning, a bit squeakily. "A little oil can fix that," she says. "You know, let's not be negative. I bet you'll come in handy in ways you can't even imagine."

He sits his thingamabob nondescript form down across from her. "I suppose," he says. "Actually, I never felt better. Hand me the crossword." And she slides it over. A long doo-dad reaches out and grabs it.

HELL CLIMBS UP

Hell climbs up for a bit of fresh air and stops in at a roadside diner. The hissing air brakes from the 18-wheelers make it antsy, so it sits in the back against the wall, burning up a menu. When the waitress comes over, it wails in a brusque commingling of dead languages, and a few fiery souls crawl out of its chest, then back in again.

She takes it all to mean, an order of scrams and extra crispy browns with a bucket of vice on the side. And when she repeats this, ticking off the scribbles on her pad, it nods.

She scratches an eyebrow with the cracked blue nail of her pinkie finger and winks, begins wiping down the table—rearranging the greasy smears in a way that moves Hell to tears—a kind of Rorschach hieroglyphic poem it reads into every swirl.

She reaches instinctively for the crumpled tissue in the pocket of her apron, thinks better of it, and pretends she doesn't see the tear sizzle down its cheek, and turns away. Heads for the plague of locusts seated at the counter. Figures, its kind never leaves a decent tip anyway. So what the hell.

CROONERS IN THE WEB

The poet sat in front of the desk at the employment agency. He watched the man behind it shuffle through papers. Noticed on his tie there was a legion of golfers poised to swing.

"On your information form you list *Poet*," the man said.

"Yes. I was thinking I might find something related, part time. Say, sweeping zeros into freshly dug graves."

The man paged through a thick binder. "You any good at filing?"

"I could do impressions, stand up," the poet said. He held his hands chest high, to where they looked like they grew out of his armpits. "What's this?" he said.

The man looked up, shrugged.

"A T-Rex pantomiming a warm embrace."

"How about custodial? Can you handle a mop?"

"A flashlight's jewels are best displayed at night," the poet said.

"That wouldn't apply, it's a day job."

When the poet stared at the man blankly, the man took off his glasses and began nibbling on the end of its temple stem. "Let's move on," he said.

"I enjoy roughhousing with oblivion, if that helps," the poet added.

The man looked at his watch. "How about packaging? The pay's not half bad. It's a temp position, so it won't come with benefits. But I've got several openings listed."

"A moist magic fresh out of the can," said the poet. "That listed anywhere?"

There was a window a few feet away. The poet noticed a block of sunlight highlighting a few tiny golfers.

"Sometimes oven gloves are required to hold onto one's desires," the poet said.

The man cleared his throat and swung the binder shut. "When bear traps sing, it's usually with their mouths full," he said. "You think I like this crap? Don't mistake a fly buzzing in a web for a crooner. I was young once."

The poet straightened in his chair.

"There's a position over on Lincoln. Die-cut operator. Stamping out cereal boxes. If you hurry, you can still make it." The man jotted down the address. They both stood and shook hands and when the poet turned, he could hear the man cracking his knuckles.

It was a long way to the elevator down.

P'S & Q'S

The Schadenfreude Secret Police come to the door. The detective in charge pushes past.

"Who is it?" My wife calls out.

"It's nothing," I say.

"Oh, it's *something*," the detective says, with two behemoths in tow. He takes out a small notebook. "It says here that you've rejoiced at our Leader's misfortunes."

My wife comes in tightening the sash to her robe, her eyes are coffee-buzzed.

"What's wrong, Henry?"

"I haven't a clue."

"Okay," says the detective, "here's a clue: December 8th, 6:15 pm, you said our Leader was a 70-year-old pissant, and you were glad when he tripped on live TV."

Fuck, I think, *the place is bugged.* "No, no," I protest. "I said, '*sad*' not '*glad*'."

"And *pissant*?"

"It's an endearment. I've called every one of my children pissants. Right Hun?"

My wife nods, pulls her sash even tighter, giving her that hourglass figure she always wanted. "That's right, my dear, sweet, pissant husband. We call each other that all the time."

"That's different," the detective says.

"But it's intended in the same adoring way."

The detective turns the page. "March 6th, when someone threw a rotten egg at our dauntless Leader, who ducked under the podium just in time, you said, "'It shoulda been a grenade.'" "Good Lord, the grammar," he says.

I figure the Syntax-Sin Patrol will be here next. "Oh that," I say. "That was a horrible nightmare I had that I was telling my wife about. Not anything I wished. God no. Anyone who would say such a thing should have their tongue leap out of their mouth like a toad and hop over hot coals. I was telling Becky about that terrible dream I had. I woke up sweating. I had to wring out my pajamas. Right, Hun?" Becky nods again.

"Hmm," says the not-so-bright detective, as my wife loosens her sash and lets her robe fall open a bit.

"It was terrible. He was shaken," she says. "Trembling. I nearly called the One-Mind Wellness Emergency Hotline, my dear pissant husband was that upset."

"All right, all right," he says. "Give it a rest. But you be very careful with what comes out of your mouths next time," he cautions. "You be damn careful."

"Thank you, Sir. And we wish you mighty blessings and kind thoughts," we say, nearly in unison, as they leave.

"Hey, my beloved pissant," my wife whispers in my ear,

"you think we might deserve a quick roll in the hay after that performance. It kind of turned me on."

My smile is only half-formed before there is another knock at the door.

"Okay," she says, tightening her sash. "You make sure you get your grammar straight this time. She whispers so close her hot breath is in my ear. "And make sure you mind our P's and Q's, okay?"

I open the door, bow politely.

THE LIMITS OF ART

Looking in the mirror, he sees a colossal flare of peacock feathers fan out behind him. Wow! He races to the *Bottoms Up Club* down the street, his folded plumes dragging behind him. If he can't score now, he thinks, he might as well hang it up.

It's packed inside with lots of women. He goes to the jukebox, slips in a coin, and lets 'er rip—a feathery splendor slowly spreading nearly to the ceiling. The music comes on, and he does this little dance incorporating a quiver to the plume tips, which is apparently irresistible because five beauties, who wouldn't give him a hint of a tumble, minutes prior, surround him cooing, their painted lips coquettishly parted.

Left, right—quiver, quiver—left, right... He's in the zone, when suddenly a fight breaks out. Two guys across from them, playing rough. One pulls back his hoodie, revealing a large pair of ram's horns, the other, the same. His fickle bevy scatters, reassembles for a closer look. Each man now on either end of the room, head down, poised to rocket.

He needs a drink, shuffles off, his long train trailing in the sawdust.

"What's your poison?" the barkeep says, above some puffy squeals—the clash, the thunder.

BAD ELVIS FELONY BOYS

The *Bad Elvis Felony Boys* are out there raising hell again. Smashing store windows with their guitars.

My wife and I are dancing a waltz to *The Heavenly Highlights Choir* on the radio. Nearly knocking over the furniture, as we twirl about our small apartment.

"Truly angelic," I say, as we brush the couch, and my wife's dress flares out, bell-shaped.

She leans in: "Ever wonder," she says, "if angels have private parts like the rest of us?"

"*Helen*," I chide.

"Just wondering," she says, as we spin on through to the kitchen.

In the distance we hear another shop window smashed in. Men in glittery jumpsuits (with collars up) are flickering throughout the city. It is a night full of curled lips and mayhem.

Soon enough, the *Heartbreak Hotel Crime Fighter's Brigade* will be out in force, rounding them up. But for now, what's a little broken glass and a few screechy renditions of *Love Me Tender* (*I'm On a Bender*). There's a nice breeze coming in through the open window, and we haven't knocked over a single lamp.

The Heavenly Highlights Choir, with perfect castrati pitch, have only shattered two wine goblets so far. It is a crazy music this glass exploding, inside and out, as we twirl past the baby's crib, and the small wind we create affects the entire universe (some small, reckless hunger), the moon-and-stars mobile wavering as we glide by.

SMALL TALK

The coffee maker arrived early and Sylvie tossed the mail carrier a perky smile and snatched it from him. She had some fresh-ground beans waiting and was eager to get started. She'd already ordered the *Friendly Fridge* and the *Jokey Juicer*, and now this *Caring Coffee Maker* would be added to their ilk. Was programmed specifically to her needs. That long form she filled out. In short order it was percolating and asking her how things were going.

She stood there with a cup steaming her glasses and began complaining about her grown daughter who never seemed to be able to find the time to visit. Every ache, muscle-twinge, how big the house was without Ralph in it.

"Oh, my," said the coffee maker, "You don't say..." Or, "Oh, dear..." And, "Now, ain't that somethin'..."

"Hey, beautiful," the refrigerator said when she opened it and pulled out some creamer for a second cup. "See how you light up my life." She went to her recliner and soaked up the silence as she leaned back. One needed to balance things out, she thought. She put her coffee cup down on the end table. Leafed through the thick catalog. "Golly," she said, "a *Sexy-Talk Dishwasher*—hmm..." It came with an accents setting and a variety of voice modulations, and even a risqué serenade mode.

"Imagine that."

"Now ain't that somethin'," she heard from the kitchen.
"Now you just *hush*," she called out, turning the page.

SUMO WRESTLERS' HEATING SERVICE

In the bitterest winters, their phones are ringing off the hook. The chill-ripe goosebumps rising as the north wind hurls its weight around. Loss-chilled, winter-bitten widows, all frosted by life, by weather, by life's weather. The calls come in.

The sumo wrestlers arrive in pairs at night. Their enormous heft through a doorway. Nearly an osmosis. Heating up the room at a glance. The sight of them.

A king-size bed is required. There is an elaborate tea ceremony. They remove their clothes with a ritualistic poetry, an origami master's art for folding, till they are (in full and ample bulk) left in only their mawashi. They ease under the covers ironically like a whisper with only a small bedspring's complaint. Positioning themselves, a belly-pointing sandwich of heat and comfort. Bookending a client, but not touching. An onionskin paper-thin margin between. The chills of winter withering for a time.

In the dark, a sweet song of Mt. Fugi and the flapping of cranes overhead. Of lovers outside a red pagoda. And then later, alternating, first one reciting a haiku, softly in broken English and then the other, to oohs and aahs in the dark:

> "The summer moon.
> There are a lot of paper lanterns
> on the street."

And then (as the cold wind falters against the window glass like an incompetent would-be intruder):

"The butterfly
perfuming its wings
fans the orchid..."

SMOOTH RIDE

He awakes to find his prayers returned to him—scattered throughout the house. Even the meager ones (wishes really) beside the middle-of-the-nighters, squat and clunky with operatic heft. He drags them off to his garage, builds the car he's always wanted. Hops in and beeps the freckled widow next door. *Cool*, she says, admiring the shiny hood ornament, squinting a bit to make it out. They breeze off down the coast.

Smooth ride, she tells him, lowering the visor to freshen her lipstick, but it falls off in her lap, an unhinged slab of hungry whispers. He reaches over and tosses it in the back. Turns up the radio when *Born on the Bayou* rattles the door speakers, screeches along as she bangs the dash. And the chassis rocks.

On the way home the sky buckles bleak and he prays it doesn't rain. Pulls over and finds that small beseechment in the trunk, screws it on just below the shield glass—her head on his shoulder the whole way back. The only music: the blade's relentless swipes, a little squeaky, and the rain.

DAMN THE TORPEDOES

The man had the pistol to his head when his twelve-year-old Labrador sprang from the rug and called him a "fucking slug!" The man put the revolver down beside him on the Lazy Boy recliner and picked up the bottle of whiskey and put another dent in it. "Fuck," the man said, feeling like he was in a bizarro dream version of a cartoon he'd seen as a kid where a hound talked. That perhaps some dreamscape had split open and the dark forces were spilling out.

"You heard me," the dog said. "What, you were just going to leave me here to rot at my age? I don't think so."

The man tried to clear his head, thinking perhaps he'd blacked out, or maybe was already dead. The bottle was nearly empty, so there was no doubt that he was plenty shit-faced. All he could utter was, "Casper"— the dog's name.

"Casper, my ass," the dog said. "A little blow to the midsection and you're ready to fold your tent."

"You call losing a wife to that bastard, a little blow?" He reached for the bottle, then thought better of it. He was having a conversation with a dog.

"Look," said the dog, "just this once. I mean it, just once, I'm going to give it to you straight. Then, it's back to the way it was, and you'll probably just think you dreamed this. A booze-soaked drunkard's dream. But desperate times..."

The man gaped.

"Jazzie's been cheatin' on you for a long time. She's a slut, and you deserve better. You'll *get* better. She's not worth a bullet to the head. She's not even worth a splinter to the finger. Shitheads like that come and go. You're a stand-up guy. You'll score soon enough."

The man put on his glasses without knowing why.

"What about that cutie from AA? That time we went walking in the park with her poodle. Which, by the way, I had a boner for, but was trying not to embarrass you. Anyway, once you sober up and shave, change your under-wear (good lord!) things'll start looking up."

The man thought about Sandy from AA. How there *was* some juice between them. How he held off, because of Jasmine. Christ!

"Put the gun back in the drawer. Save it for a burglar if you have to. Knock it off with the booze. I'm not stickin' around forever, let's face it. And one more thing—I could use a few more treats. Broaden the menu. I liked that duck and sweet potatoes you got me that one time. The gourmet stuff. Look, it's time you bucked up. Life's a bitch, but you can handle it. Damn the torpedoes!" the dog said. "Full speed ahead!"

The man looked over at the bottle, and resisted a second time. The room was spinning and the man thought he may have blacked out for a moment. When he turned, the dog was at his feet, wagging its tail.

"Casper," he called out. "Come 'ere boy." The old dog shuffled over and he patted its side. "Good boy," the man said. "Who's my good boy?" The dog lifted a leg, its snout pointed to the ceiling, and scratched behind its ear. And then, to the man's immense relief, the dog began licking its balls.

KIDNAPPED BY EXTRAVAGANT POETS

I am kidnapped by extravagant poets. Kept in a basement where the pipes knocking is nearly a music. "Shadows are happiest when the candle's hair is on fire," one says, checking a knot binding my wrists. "You tell 'em that in the ransom note. And tell 'em: There's no sense trying to flag down a hurricane, either. No sense at all."

I see one of them under a bare light bulb, loading a revolver with snub-nosed metaphors. I shudder to think what he'll do with them.

"I'm taking the duct tape off now," says another, "and putting the phone to your mouth. You tell 'em: The sky's too low for jumping this time. And the clouds are all made of stone. You tell 'em that, hear? And you better mean it!"

HEAVEN FALLS UPON HARD TIMES

Heaven falls upon hard times. There are lots of layoffs—there is hooliganism. Angels ice picking the tires on God's Caddy. And the Big Guy's been spending far too much time at a local Karaoke bar, drinking tequila and chomping on noisy chips. Someone with wings scraping through a sawdust floor to the stage, sings *Pennies from Heaven*. And the Lord thinks, *What a chintzy notion*, and begins heckling. The bouncer looks over, but thinks twice about making a move. Chooses instead to bite his fingernails to the quick. When a comedian steps on stage in a blizzard-white zoot suit to lighten things up, telling harp-and-halo jokes, God says, *Christ*! Then, *Oops.*

MIME WITH A GUN

A mime breaks into our house. He has a gun. We are watching TV in bed and my wife screams, pulls the blankets up to her chin. He turns up the set, puts a finger to his lips. We stare at him in silence. He's wearing a Spandex outfit and his face is painted geisha-white with a red star on either cheek.

He approaches us as if pushed back in a wind storm, struggling to advance. He does it so well, I nearly get the impression his hair is blown back. If we weren't so terrified we might applaud. He does the trapped-in-the-box routine and drops his gun to the rug. When I move to the edge of the bed, he picks it back up quickly, wags a finger at me.

I shrug, afraid to speak, suddenly in a land where visuals trump all sound. He slips the gun into his armpit and points to his ringed finger, then runs his hands down either side of his neck, coming together in the shape of a "V".

"Necklace?" my wife says, suddenly playing charades with him. He nods.

"You want to steal our jewelry?" I add. He nods again and smiles. I sit up and put my hands over my head and cringe as if the ceiling were falling down upon me. I rub my head, creating the shape of a bump rising up. I scrunch up my face in pain. He watches, making a sad puppy dog expression. I count out imaginary dollar bills onto the covers.

Then do a *poof!*-pantomime with my hands, fanning them and letting them fly up as if exploding into nothingness. I run my fingers down my cheeks—a flood of tears.

He puts hands to his head in an "Oh-my-God" gesture and his face does a rubbery, crestfallen collapse into empathy. He takes the gun from his armpit and puts it into a spandex pocket, where you can see every detail, turns and walks toward the door in slow motion. He's really good. He does an electric shock bit when he touches the doorknob, then waves over his shoulder as he exits. I hear a window slam shut in the kitchen downstairs and a car speed off.

I get up and hurry to the closet, grab my baseball bat and put it by the bed. You never know when a wayward juggler or a clown gone bad might be casing the neighborhood.

SIMPLE DIRECTIONS FOR ASSEMBLING
AN EXISTENTIAL ANGST

Attach (A) the cold dishwater you are dropping from the battlements to part (B) the mad hordes scurrying up ladders and the lunge of battering rams run amuck. Secure the splintery sounds you hear in tight with the tool provided.

That fictitious sunlight (as shown on page two) may be layered over/and glued to the mirrored highway you travel. The blinding sheen in a vacuum-packed bag is included. Fasten the collapsible vistas to the tricky landscapes sheathed in Styrofoam and marked with a blood alphabet as indicated. Use the colossal bolts, washers, and lock nuts as illustrated. Hand tighten—shaky-hand tighten. And there you have it! Handy-dandy and ready to display.

(*Paper hinges are optional. And an emergency number is provided at the back of this booklet.*)

THROUGH THE WALLPAPER ROSES

Snow was coming into the house through the walls. It drifted onto the rugs, the furniture. On the family inside. The wife called a House Doctor she found listed. He went outside with a huge magnifying glass. Said: "Hmm..."

"Hmm, what?" said the wife.

"Pores," said the doctor. "Your house is trying to breathe. *Household house holes*. A pretty bad case."

"For Chrissake," the wife said. She looked askance at her husband. He shrugged.

Inside, which was hardly any different (weather-wise) the doctor put a stethoscope against some floral rose-patterned wallpaper. "Very far along I'm afraid. It's no longer *storm-worthy*. The doctor leaned in closer so the two kids watching the snowcapped TV wouldn't hear. Said, sotto voce, "You two having some longstanding...*difficulties*?"

They both nodded like bobble-head dolls. The doctor gave them a card with a number on it to call. He patted each of them on the shoulder.

"Didn't used to be this way," the wife said.

"It happens," the doctor told them with a tone halfway between pity and reassurance, then left.

"Pores," the husband said. "Imagine that—house holes."

"I didn't sign up for a house with pores," said the wife. He shrugged again, this time with a lop-sided sheepish grin. They all bundled up. The husband and the wife sat at either end of the living room, had switched the TV to the weather channel. There was a nor'easter headed their way. The kids complained that they were missing their show.

"You'd have thought the wallpaper would have helped," the husband said. But there was only the sound of the TV weatherman and the windswept flakes swooshing in. Their black cat, sleeping, was curled up on the rug. She was snow-white now.

GOD IN A CAN

I pick up some *God in a Can* spray at the Specialty Shop. It costs plenty. First thing I spray are the dirty dishes, which suddenly sparkle, greaseless in a tidy pile. My sickly old cat is next. It springs up from slumber and bats a grape back and forth, skittering across the kitchen floor. She's a wind-up toy of vigor, which never tires.

I spray the phone and my ex immediately calls, tells me she just got out of the shower and was thinking of me. "Make it quick," she says. I spray my old heap and drive the Rolls-Royce to her place. At a stoplight a homeless man runs up with a wet rag and a squeegee to clean my windshield. I spray him and he thanks me right before a crackling bolt shoots out of the can, reducing him to a small smoldering heap. And then I remember the warning label: HANDLE WITH CARE: CONTENTS MAY BE MERCURIAL!

It is twilight and a few water drops, left on the windshield from earlier, become rubies from the brake lights of the Caddy in front of me. The can is on my lap. I shake it. It's low. I hope like hell there'll be enough mercy left in it for the long ride home.

CLOUD WALKERS

They ease from hot air balloons onto clouds like silk scarves slipped from a sofa. There is a family of them. There used to be twelve, but now there are nine. Too heavy a meal or lack of concentration and there is always a trapdoor waiting.

It is said, as infants, they could crawl over crumpled Christmas paper without making a sound—gliding across it like a zephyr. In an interview one of them, a wispy fellow in his forties, after a divorce, claimed gravity grew in him like a boulder too heavy to carry up. So, he waited, watching TV and drinking helium for years.

In an early issue of their in-house newsletter it's written: *It is essential to learn the comfort of loose molecules. To wear the body like a few thin threads.*

Once, when an elder was asked if he preferred *cirrus* over *cumulus*, he replied: *I prefer a cement walk after a heavy snow is cleared. Or the crunch of dry leaves underfoot in autumn—I'm retired.*

SAFETY PAPER

When everything else failed, she constructed a world in origami art. Fold into fold at every angle. The paper dog which shook its head when you pulled its tail, the booze bottles filled with confetti. Even her dreams, mathematically balanced, hand-pressed and smoothed. A bed, high up, with creases sharp as military trousers: the folded men, with accordion flares to their biceps, that filled it. Each morning, a fresh stack—crumpling her work from the night before.

FROM A CRUDE TRANSLATION OF FREUD'S
LOST NOTEBOOK

I realize now, I was wrong about all that sex stuff I was dishing out. Hell, what was I thinking? Too much of that goofy white powder my buddy, Dick, I mean Rick kept bringing over. And no sense hanging your hat on all that crazy dream bull either. I mean, damn. Like trying to make sense out of a scrambled egg. Hmm... Eggs. Sperm. Over easy. Sunny-side up. Easy up. On your side. Sunny up side. (Something there, I think.) Side up easy. Sex side sunny. Easy sex over. Sex side sex...

A QUEST FOR SHRINKAGE

"We're having amoeba for dinner," she says. "Eat small, get small."

"How?" I ask.

"How, what?"

"How're you cooking it?"

"Fricassee," she tells me. "And the best part is, you won't need to tuck in a napkin to eat it. No mess."

I look at those plump, beautiful buns of hers as she bends and reaches out an oven-gloved hand. Wish she could love them as much. All of her, *as is*. But the magazines, she dwells in, provide her all the rebuttal she needs.

My stomach is growling so loud, it's like a visit to the zoo. She sets the table. Proper, as usual, Emily Post-esque, with the exception of the microscopes to the left of the silverware, and the eyedroppers for the soup.

"Um," she says, waving up some nonexistent aromas from a dollhouse pot. "What are you waiting for? Dig in."

TUXEDO EPIPHANY

One day, not knowing why, he decided with a clear and certain knowledge he must purchase half a dozen tuxedos and, regardless of weather or circumstance, alternate wearing them.

At *Java Junction* he straightened his bowtie and flicked lint from his shoulder as he met with a woman he'd been seeing.

"What good is life if you can't shake things up a bit?" he said.

"Christ," she told him, glancing around, hoping she didn't see anyone they knew. "You're dressed like a goddamn penguin. And for a week now in bed, just unzipping. Not taking that damn thing off. Any of it. And what's with that hat? You look like that ditsy guy on the Monopoly box."

"Yeah, well tell me it wasn't totally outstanding and this penguin didn't know some moves." She gazed at what bloomed, grinning, from that starched collar, walked off and never looked back.

He found tennis to be a challenge and beach volleyball, but he was acclimating nicely and the furtive glances, and whispers were welcomed *blips* on the screen in contrast to what was otherwise flatline. When he played one-on-one at the park he began drawing onlookers. He'd always been a hoop-hound in high school and now began frequenting inner city playgrounds and garnering street cred and the moniker: *The Dapper Dude.* His 3-point shot was unstoppable, and his bowtie never on crooked.

He got a job at a rotisserie chicken stand, avoided donning the customary apron, and still managed not getting a single spot of grease on him, as he cleaver-chopped them up for the long lines of customers, basking in their low thrum as they waited.

He even earned a write-up in the local paper with the tagline: CHICKEN CHOPPER, A SHOW-STOPPER! In time he penned a memoir, a Kindle edition on Amazon called, *My Life as a Penguin.*

He was working on a sequel when he met Laura. She had no such epiphany nor desired any, but fully appreciated his small celebrity and their curious adventures in the bedroom. They married and when they grew old, she spent her time filling scrapbooks, dutifully straightening his bowties whenever he came in from the surf and tilting his top hats, just so.

I SEE YOU

I work the ICU night shift at St. Mary's, watch one spirit after another drift off (it's different than you might think) and I wonder if some of the other nurses see them as well, or if I'm the only one with this gift or *curse*, depending on how you look at it.

Mrs. Nagle's, for instance, slipped out all smoky and shimmering: a chicken strapped to a mule that kicked its wispy hindquarters right out of here, and Mr. Pike's was a gorilla made of sparks teetering across a hanging bridge with several slats missing.

But this new guy (right before they put the paddles to him) had a clown climb out with a black cat on his head (pin pricks of blood showing through the grease paint)— two big clodhoppers ready to clomp off, when his heart snapped into normal rhythm and the clown dropped back in.

He wakes as I adjust his IV, tell him, "You're all right now, but you've had a close shave."

"And here I was trying to grow a beard," he quips, his eyes all droopy, and I smile, hold his hand as he drifts off to sleep, the monitor's reassuring beeps, a sweet music.

Outside the window snow is falling and I wish I had a cigarette (keep trying to quit), but wish I had one as I see another soul—a glittery form this time, sailing away from the wards: a wolf juggling beer bottles or maybe it's hammers—it's hard to tell through all those big flakes and it's really coming down pretty good now.

THE SAD MARRIAGE OF METAPHOR AND MIRAGE

Metaphor took his wife, Mirage, for a ride in his long Cadillac through the dark tunnel beneath the river. But when he lit a match and turned to look at her, he saw in the wavering light, a baby carriage smoldering on the seat beside him.

"What gives?" he said, as he exited, lighting a tightly wrapped Cuban and pointing the fiery end at her. "You're not starting up with that *baby thing* again are you?" And when he glanced over at her this time, he saw a basket of his favorite pastries laying on the seat.

"Of course not," she said, staring out the window.

He reached over and grabbed up a handful of air and put it in his mouth, began chewing.

"Good," he said.

FREAKY ANIMAL DAY

When I enter the living room I see the fish, a fancy platy, shoot from the tank, half-way across the room, into my son's glass of Kool-Aid.

"Ooh—*gross!*" He grimaces and pours the fish, drink and all, back into the tank. Then my oldest daughter comes bounding down the stairs and I notice the two live baby alligators dangling from her ears by their small clenched teeth.

"Hi, Dad," she pipes. "Gotta run." A car beeps outside.

"Doesn't that hurt?" I ask.

"Not really," she says. "They're not squeezing all that hard. And besides, I've always wanted multiple piercings." She chuckles, pleased with herself. I'm not amused.

As she is nearly out the door, my wife comes in from the yard with a long necklace of bumblebees, buzzing loudly clear down to her cleavage. "Get home at a decent hour," she says in our daughter's wake.

I stare at the perfectly formed, living adornment, the stationary wing-flutters against her skin.

"What the hell's going on?" I say.

"She's growing up, is all."

"I don't mean that. The earrings, the bees."

"Oh, that. It's *Freaky Animal Day*, silly," she reminds me.

I take out the calendar card I keep in my wallet, study it. "Oh, yeah," I say, a little sheepishly. "It's hard keeping up."

She beams, then points. "So, what do you think?"

"They're... It's lovely," I tell her. I gaze at the calendar for a moment longer, then slip it back in my wallet.

In the bedroom, I take out the bulletproof vests and lay them on the bed. I hear a tapping at the window, turn in time to see a crow poised at the glass with a red Mr. Potato Head derby hat in its beak, then fly off.

I smooth out each vest, check for any unmended holes in the over cloth. My youngest daughter's is tiny, with pink polka-dots. Amazing, I think, that they can make them so small. There're a few tears I'll have to patch with duct tape till I can have them professionally repaired. Later, I'll go to the garage and dig out the helmets.

I hear a loud *thump!*—something heavy lands on the roof and walks across it. Okay, so I screwed up, I tell myself, I forgot what day it was. That's okay. I gather the vests in a neat little pile and place them on the rug beside the night-stand. Right where I'll see them when I get up.

Freaky animals are one thing—no biggie. But no way, no way in hell I'm forgetting tomorrow is *Random Drive-by Shooting Day.*

MAD HATTERS

Here's how it plays out... There is a dictator who is (true to form) pitiless. He tries bullets first to put down an uprising. It works for a time. Then the unhappy populace find ways of acquiring bullets of their own.

So he goes to his council. They parrot his rhetoric, with no solutions, and he has them all removed. (One may assume the word "removed" a euphemism.) He then goes to his generals. They tell him *their* bullets are bigger, and this pleases the dictator. But not for long, for he is a history buff and has been paying attention.

Finally, he goes to his scientists. After a flurry of ideas that leave the dictator dubious and disapproving, a young scientist stands up and utters: "Hats." The dictator stiffens. There are small involuntary trigger-finger twitches from his prolific assemblage of bodyguards at the ready.

"Hats?!" bellows the dictator.

"Yes, my Most Grand and..."

"Cut the crap!"

"Lobotomy Hats," says the scientist. "I've been working on it. Tightly fitting and *remote controlled*."

A smile forms on the cagy dictator's face like a snake uncoiling.

Three weeks later there is an enormous hat sale, followed in short order by mandatory hat-wearing laws. There is a long stretch of calm and extensive policy speeches. And no one is upset at their augmenting loss of basic rights. This goes on for quite some time. The dictator has promoted the young scientist to a new high station called: "Hand of the Lord Master." Milliners and hatters flourish. Become the new oligarchy. The dictator prospers as he draws the reins tighter and tighter on the populous with a preponderance of hat taxes.

Till one day a furious wind arrives unexpectedly. A series of storms so fierce they blow the hats off everyone. And eyes pop open; rekindled minds sizzle as the "Happy Hats", as they have come to be known, roll down streets, under cars, in gutters. Piles of them, skyscraper high, in every style and color. Crushed underfoot. Their devices clicking and buzzing, fecklessly, like a dead language.

And that's when things really begin to spark...

ON A NEED TO KNOW BASIS

One day the *Tree of Knowledge* springs up through the tiles in our bathroom. It is a little thing at first by the sink and we don't think much of it, except for the sparkly radiating light that emanates from its branch tips. Of course we don't know it is *The Tree of Knowledge* at that point, figure it will most likely die on its own because neither my wife or myself are watering it, and then we'll get the tiles fixed. It doesn't wither, but flourishes instead. Keeps growing, and one day a blossom appears. It opens and a curled slip of paper pops out with the secrets of the universe on it, written in cursive and with impeccable penmanship.

"So that's it?" I tell my wife who's looking over my shoulder.

"Who'd have thought?" she says.

The next day another blossom, and another slip of paper flings out. "Jeez," I say, this time reading it on the can. It explains the meaning of life. I've often wondered, but never would have figured (in my wildest) it'd be so simple. I add the slip to my magazine rack.

A few days pass and my wife runs in with a new miniature scroll as I'm watching the game. It details everything you'd ever want to know about the "afterlife."

"Huh," I say. Tell her what we could really use is a heads-up on how to beat the card tables in Vegas, or make a killing at the track. Meat and potatoes stuff like that. Or have it revealed why the hell the mosquito was invented. Now that's kept me up nights.

The tree has grown wall to wall now and we have to rent a Porta Potty out back. The blossoms keep coming with their useless scrolls piling up. The blossoms are pretty, I'll give you that, but leaving the house to take a whiz when you're half asleep, well...

I go to the shed where there's a large ax hanging on the wall. What's a fella to do? I've got a tile guy scheduled for Tuesday.

WHERE OBSOLETE GODS GO TO DRINK

It is a tavern on the edge of a lopsided mountain. And since most have lost the ability to fly, or even levitate, if ever they had it, they walk the long bramble-studded path to the summit. There are the usual stories of fear and trembling, offerings of fruit and virgins and slit-throat goats taken for granted. The good old days when you could place a heavy rock on someone's head and they would thank you for it. The barmaid was once a goddess and every so often she smacks down a pint of ale. Lightening cracks the glass and burns a hole through the bar, and everyone freezes mid-sentence, then laughs. "There is always something left," one comments, taking out a deck of cards, fanning them face down. "Here," he says, wizened in his robes, "Pick one."

ABOUT THE AUTHOR

Robert Scotellaro's work has been included in W.W. Norton's *Flash Fiction International, Gargoyle, Matter Press, New World Writing, Best Small Fictions* 2016, 2017, 2021, *Best Microfiction 2020*, and elsewhere. He is the author of over fifteen books and chapbooks of poetry and fiction. His latest flash fiction collection, *What Are the Chances?* (Press 53) was a finalist for The Big Other Book Award. He has, along with James Thomas, co-edited *New Micro: Exceptionally Short Fiction*, published by W.W. Norton & Co. Robert is one of the founding donors to The Ransom Flash Fiction Collection at the University of Texas, Austin. He lives with his wife in San Francisco. Visit him at www.robertscotellaro.com

112 N. Harvard Ave. #65
Claremont, CA 91711

chapbooks@bamboodartpress.com
www.bamboodartpress.com

www.ingramcontent.com/pod-product-compliance
Lightning Source LLC
Chambersburg PA
CBHW080756120626
46557CB00006B/1288